For Marcus

Published and distributed by Bedtime Press LLC

www.bedtime.press

ISBN 978-0-9975673-1-1

Manufactured in China

Good Night Little Turtle

Story By **David Cunliffe**   Illustrated By **Tiffany Cunliffe**

It's getting very late,
it's time for some sleep.
Let's say good night to the fluffy white sheep.

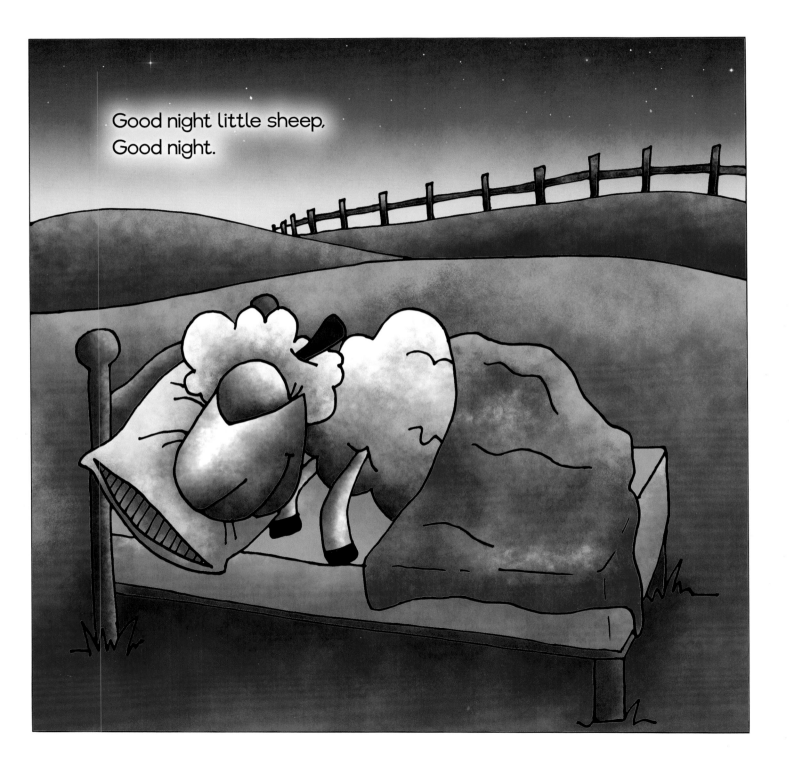

Hello little bird!
I could hardly see you at that height!
You must be tired from your flight.
Now rest your wings,
turn out the light,
and climb into your nest tonight.

Good night little bird,
Good night.

Hello little frog!
What a delight, to see you flying your red kite.
But it's getting late, and we're losing light.
So gather your things, pack them up tight,
then you can get some rest tonight.

Hello little dog!
I really like your red flashlight.
I've never seen one quite so bright.
But it's getting late, and it's almost night.
Time to rest and turn off your light.

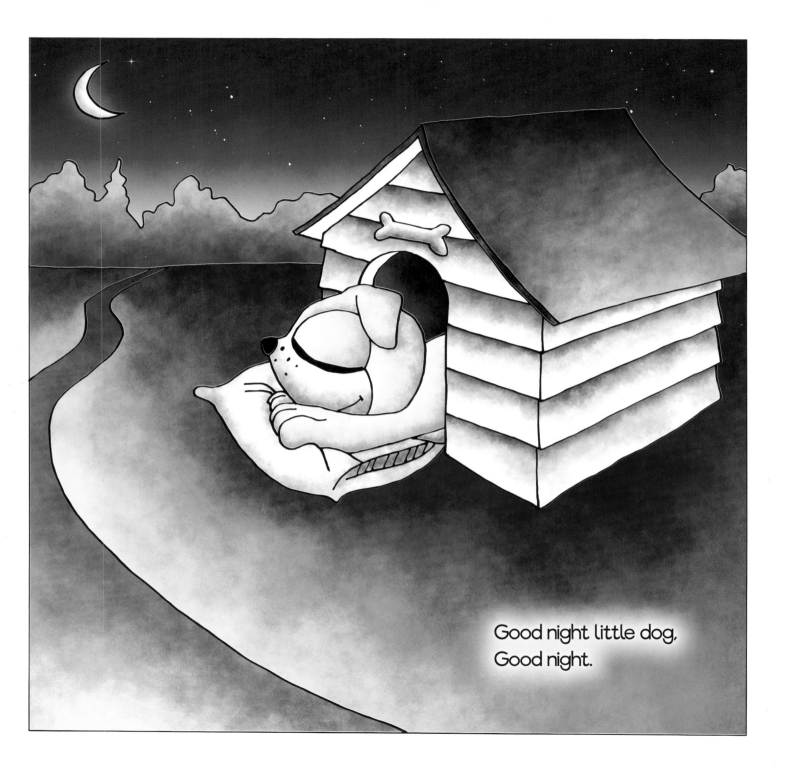

Good night little dog,
Good night.

Hello little rabbit!
It's nice to see you, fluffy white,
hopping logs this lovely night.
Time to rest your legs tonight.

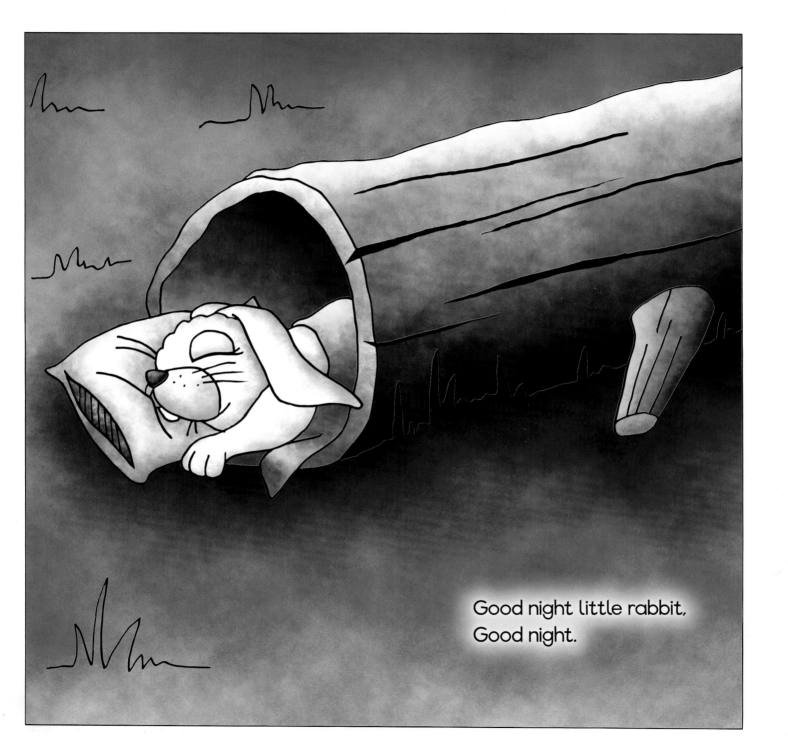

Good night little rabbit,
Good night.

Look, there's a lion, filled with fright!
Sometimes even lions get scared at night.
Don't worry my friend,
it will be all right.

Time to brush my teeth,
get them clean and bright,
then get all cozy and turn out the light.

There was a little tiger,
that loved to play.
He would run and wrestle,
and play all day.

After swimming in the pond,
and climbing in the trees,
his tiger parents said,
"Come to dinner please!"

He ate his dinner,
then he played some more.
He jumped up and down,
and he slid across the floor...

And when it got late,
his tiger Mom said,
"Okay little tiger,
it's time for bed."

Good night little tiger,
Good night.

Now I've had a story,
time to turn out the light.
I saw all my friends,
to say good night.
I've brushed my teeth,
and I'm tucked in tight,
and I know I'll sleep just fine tonight.

Good night little turtle,
Good night.

www.bedtime.press